AF295162

novum pro

Folorunso G. Makinde

ON THE
BRIDGE

novum pro

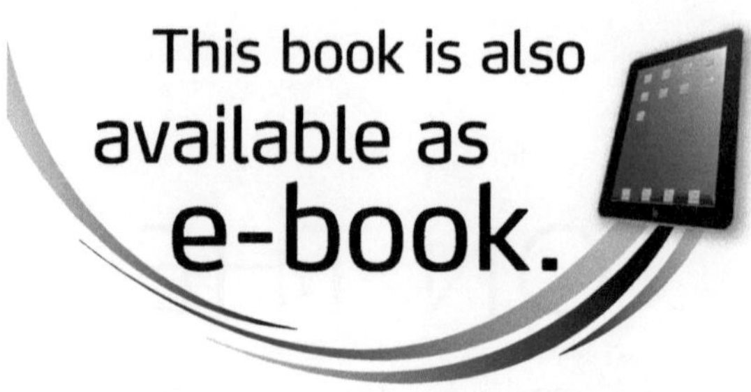

© 2023 novum publishing

ISBN 978-3-99064-111-8
Editing: Hugo Chandler, BA
Cover photo:
Martinmark | Dreamstime.com
Cover design, layout & typesetting:
novum publishing

www.novum-publishing.co.uk

CHAPTER 1

It was a day like any other in Lagos, southwestern Nigeria. People were going about their normal everyday business. The traffic was heavy as was always the case at this time of the morning. The buses, like massive cranes painted yellow and showing signs of ageing, were full of workers trying to get to their places of work on time. The roads were full of vehicles – some fairly used and others quite old. In fact, many of them looked like the work of a struggling local motor mechanic trying to make a living by putting hard-worn metal parts together to look like a home-made vehicle.

Appearances can be very deceptive though. These vehicles always look as if they could barely travel a mile before they broke down. However, motor car engines never died here. If it couldn't be made to work as the single unit it once was, the parts could be made to work as separate units put together after undergoing some form of local metamorphosis. Many of the vehicles that were nicknamed Tokunbos (from abroad) were imported second hand vehicles that had failed road-worthiness tests in their respective countries of origin. The luxury and fairly new cars usually had two passengers – the driver sitting in the front and the owner sitting in one corner at the back.

There were no quiet moments on the bridge. The vehicle engines were always kept running even though the long traffic queue moved very slowly. That was the best way. You couldn't afford to be slow in moving your vehicle because if you were slow, another vehicle would overtake you, making your journey even longer. Then there were vehicles whose owners couldn't afford to turn off the engine because it might take longer and a lot of effort to get the engine restarted.

The newspapers vendors blew their 'Vuvuzela' hooters' just to get attention and the hawkers were always on the move, approaching vehicle drivers and passengers to offer them their wares. Some drivers ignored them but many did business with them. Business dealings on the bridge are governed by an unspoken rule: you must have the goods in your hands before parting with your money. If you didn't have the correct amount to pay, you had to first get the change and the goods before parting with your money. That was how business was done on the bridge. It was the smarter way to do business on the bridge if you didn't want to take the risk of parting with your money, getting nothing in return.

The noise of the stomping of uncountable feet of people walking on the bridge was drowned-out by all the other noise.

Every now and again, a motorist tries to jump the traffic queue. 'Bastard!' shouts another driver who is abiding by the rules of the queue. 'Olosi!' (wretched person), shouts a bus conductor at another car trying to jump the queue. However, the bus driver soon took a chance, also attempting to jump the queue. The bus passengers were very uneasy about this as the driver's action put their lives at risk. Their bus might collide with another vehicle or they might be stopped by the police who are half-heartedly try-ing to enforce the law, but who would ignore the law if a driver bribes them with enough money. Many commuters know the game. They know that the police are not well paid and will do anything to supplement their meagre income. The commuters always have some money (lower denominations of the currency) for this purpose.

Upon the offering and receiving of bribes, the police might even help the vehicles by clearing the way. Therefore, while the main concern of the passengers was about not being involved in an ac-cident, the greater fear was that of having the bus driver and the conductor being stopped by the police and having to part with their hard-earned cash. The going rate was determined by what you were stopped for and where you are stopped. The amount you would pay was higher when you were caught doing something bad or something which appeared to be bad when you were stopped at a routine police checkpoint, probably set up for the purpose of collecting money from passing vehicles. If you were unlucky enough to be stopped in a very quiet area, you might need to pay more. Therefore, the usual response from the passengers when their bus driver decided to jump the traffic queue was always some grumbles, a sigh and a silent prayer. It usually worked. Accidents were not often caused by such behaviour by bus drivers. There is a popular saying: "If you can drive in Lagos, you can drive anywhere in the world."

The queue was moving unusually slow that day. One driver was contemplating whether or not to jump the queue.

'Don't do it dear. Let's wait,' said his wife.

'But you know dear, we're going to be very late,' the husband replied.

'I know dear. But let's wait.'

The husband listened to the advice of his wife. He decided not to jump the queue that day.

Another time, he might not have listened but the meeting they were to attend that day was not that important. They could afford to be late. Heeding the advice of his wife today turned out to be one of the best decisions the husband ever made in his life as a few moments later, the sound of gunshots was heard coming not too far ahead on the bridge. This caused a commotion among the commuters. Everyone ducked. Some of those walking along took to their heels. To avoid witnessing a terrible incident, one needs to run ('Koju ma ribi, ese loogun e'). More sounds of gunshots were heard and then followed by shouts and screams. There was commotion everywhere. Pedestrians started to run away from where the gunshots were. Some joined them simply because they saw others running even though they didn't even know what they were running from or where they were running to. Some vehicles tried to make a U-turn in an effort to get away from the bridge as fast as possible. This resulted in more traffic jams. The sound of gunshots was not unfamiliar in Lagos. It is usually due to one of two things; armed robbers are operating in the area or police are operating there. However, there had been no signs of police vehicles or police operating on the bridge that morning, as no vehicle trying to jump the queue had been stopped.

The commuters' biggest fear was realising that armed robbers were operating on the bridge. Young men performing armed robbery were usually well-armed and didn't take nonsense from anyone. It appeared to be a well-planned operation as they usually are – the group's two vehicles were close behind each other in the queue. The one behind had moved forward as if it were about to overtake the other, but then it stopped suddenly, blocking the way of any other vehicle from moving while the operation went on.

One of the armed robbers, Bobby got out of the car, shot into the air and shouted, "Stay in your cars and don't move!" He was carrying an AK 47 in his right hand. The two drivers of the vehicles belonging to the armed robbers stayed put. The other members of the group got out of the two cars; each carrying an automatic rifle. Two members of the group Ade and Ben stood beside the two vehicles, each facing different directions keeping close watch on the movement of people around them. The remaining six members of the group, each with an automatic rifle split themselves into two groups of three to form the raiding party. The two groups moved in opposite directions, with each group moving from one vehicle to another, demanding that the passengers hand over their valuables. Bobby led the group heading north while Imam led the group heading south. The people occupying the vehicles knew that the armed robbers must not be toyed with. They meant business and would shoot to kill if you do not comply with their demands.

Something like this could only happen in this country. How could anyone in their right mind choose to carry out an armed robbery on a bridge, knowing that they could easily be cut off and arrested? However, this is not like any other country. This is Nigeria and this is Lagos. The robbers knew that they were seldom disturbed by the police. Therefore, they more or less had free rein to do as they wanted. They could afford to take their time. This was not the first time they had performed such an operation and in fact it was not the first time they had held up a bridge. Meanwhile, the operation continued unhindered.

CHAPTER **2**

At the Lagos Central Police Station, calls were coming in. "There is an armed robbery taking place on the bridge."

"Oga (master), dem (they) say a gang is holding up a bridge in the North West of Lagos." The police constable repeated the information to the boss, Peter Jang.

"And what do they want us to do? Tell them to ring the mainland police station. They are closer. It is their responsibility not ours," replied the boss.

Mr Peter Jang was a decorated superintendent in the police. He had been in the Nigerian Police Force for over twenty years. He was also a married father of four. He took his job very seriously and always tried his best within the scope allowed, despite the scant resources provided by the government. His efforts had been recognised which was the reason why he was promoted to the rank of superintendent. He was a very honest police officer and though he realized that many officers were involved in corrupt practices, he tried not to get involved. He did nothing to stop them either as this might jeopardize his police career. A policeman did not have to join in if he or she didn't want to, but they didn't try to stop others' corrupt practices as every officer always knew a senior officer who knew a more senior officer who benefited from corrupt practices.

Corruption is endemic not only within the Nigerian Police Force but within the whole Nigerian society. Many governments had come and gone having made promises to tackle corruption before coming to power but many if not all of them still ended up being corrupt themselves. None of the so-called big shot had ever been prosecuted. One politician would accuse others of stealing public money but that was as far as it went.

There was an unspoken practice among politicians not to prosecute any big shots. 'Steal as much as you can while you are in power but don't prosecute the previous government.' This was the rule. How could any new government prosecute his or her colleagues. Anyway they had been waiting in the queue for a long time just to take their turn at stealing public money. This is their chance. They not only didn't want to waste their time pursuing the previous government but they also knew that once they left the seat of power, they didn't want to worry about being prosecuted themselves either. So, corruption becomes a vicious circle. The justice system is not completely out of what was going on either. Everyone understood the game.

"Sir, apparently the robbers are close to this side of the bridge," said the officer manning the calls.

"Do I need to repeat myself? Tell them they should ring the mainland police station. It is their responsibility. No one wants to die. I have a wife and four children," Mr Jang muttered. The other officers agreed. They knew that the armed robbers were usually well armed and in fact usually better armed than the police. The police authority had been asking for better equipment from the government for a long time but their demands had fallen on deaf ears.

"Oga say make you ring the mainland police station, dem for responsible for the bridge," the junior officer told the person on the other end of the phone; but the calls never stopped coming in.

"Oga, there have been many calls now and they are still coming in."

"Tell them we no get weapon."

"Sorry, we no get weapon. Ring the mainland police station, maybe they get weapon." The officer responded to the caller.

Meanwhile on the bridge, the armed robbery operation continued. The occupants of each vehicle waited patiently and quietly wait for their turn.

"Wetin (what) you get inside the car?" asked one of the armed robbers, looking sternly at the driver of the vehicle.

"Nothing sir." The lady sitting in the back seat replied. She was the owner of the vehicle. The driver stayed silent, allowing the questions to be directed towards the lady owner. He was not the owner of the vehicle; just the hired driver.

"What!" one of the robbers barked.

"This is my bag. There is my purse, my GSM … nothing else …" The lady responded as she handed over her personal belongings.

"Put your necklace inside and your wrist watch." The robber held out a bag.

"Okay sir," she complied without any hesitation. The people knew not to mess around with the armed robbers. When those guys held guns in their hands, they held life and death. As much as you loathed what they were doing, you'd better give them the respect that the guns they are holding deserve.

"What about you lover boy?" shouted one of the robbers at the man sitting beside the lady at the back of the car. "What's in your pocket and don't waste my time."

"I … I …"

"Step out of the car". The man stepped out of the car trembling. He handed over all the money in his pocket, together with his gold watch, necklace and a mobile phone.

"What have you got in the boot?"

"Nothing," the lady in the car replied.

"I wasn't talking to you. I was talking to him," said one of the robbers who asked the question.

"Nothing … I don't know," the man said, visibly shaking.

"Open it make I see." The man took the key from the driver, but as he was about to move towards the boot of the car, one of the robbers snatched the car key from him and opened the car boot.

"Wow… What have we got here?"

"What is it Small Boy?" one of the robbers asked, from the other side of the trunk of the car. In the trunk of the car was a suitcase.

"What is the combination?"

"It is mm … mm …"

"There's nothing inside, just paper work," replied the lady, sitting inside the car.

"What is the combination?" one of the robbers repeated.

"247 … sir," the man replied. Using the combination that he had just been given, Small Boy opened the suitcase. The suitcase contained a large sum of money.

"Wow! I thought you said there was nothing in the boot," Small Boy asked.

"I didn't say that I only said I didn't know," the man replied. Small Boy turned his face towards the lady in the car. The look on the face of the other robbers changed.

"You lied to us," one of the robbers said with a stern look at the man from whom they had taken the key from.

"Sorry sir, I didn't know there was a suitcase in the boot," the man said.

"How did you know about the suitcase? No one mentioned any suitcase."

"It does not belong to me, I swear."

"How did you know the combination to open the suitcase if you didn't know about the suitcase," another robber said, looking at the man.

The other armed robber nearer the car turned towards the lady sitting in the car. "You lied to us."

"I beg you sir. I didn't …" The other robber called Imam opened fire and shot her dead. Small boy shot and killed the driver inside the car.

Imam then turned the gun on the man and shot him dead too. Small Boy picked up the suitcase but, as they moved away from the car, Imam said: "Allahu Akbar."

"Why did you say that?" asked Adio the third member of the group.

"What?"

"Doesn't that mean 'God is great'?" asked Adio.

"Yeah," replied Imam.

"Are you referring to the same God Almighty or another God?"

"The same one and only God Almighty," replied Imam.

"But you just destroyed the work of the hand of that God and you followed it with 'God is great,'" added Adio.

"Yeah! That's what we usually say. Mm … You won't understand," explained Imam.

"Well, God will forgive the 'We'," said Adio.

The killings were witnessed by the occupants of the next vehicle and it must have sent shivers down their spine so they did not hesitate to cooperate fully with the robbers and in fact cooperated more than could have been expected. They handed over everything they had on them, including their jewellery, money and other valuables. They opened the boot of their vehicle for the robbers to see and check. The robbers continued to move from one vehicle to another without fear or hesitation or any inhibition.

Meanwhile, at the police station a call came in for the superintendent of police. "Sir, Madam want to speak to you."

"Tell her I'm busy. I will call her back later. I have told her many times not to call me when I am at work unless it is an emergency." Superintendent Jang had warned his wife many times not to call him at the office and in particular when the issue could be discussed when he returned home unless it couldn't wait.

"Sir it is not madam, it is 'The Madam'".

"What does she want?" he murmured. "I'll take it in my office," he said. The call was put through to Superintendent Jang's office.

"Hi darling. What is it? I am very busy. There's a hold up on the bridge by armed robbers," he added.

"Yes I know. This is the reason why I'm calling. We are caught up in it, me and your boy," said Aunty Esther at the other end of the phone.

"What!" Mr Jang exclaimed, a look of fright visible on his face. He moved toward the door to his office and closed it. "You were supposed to be going home," he said. "What are you doing on the bridge at this time of the day?"

Mr Jang although married with four children, had been having an extramarital relationship with Esther, a lady he had met at a friend's birthday party. The affair had been going on for about two years now. Mrs Jang was unaware of this. Mr Jang had not gone home last night. He had stayed at the officers' quarters allocated to high-ranking officers. The quarters were not very far from the police station where Superintendent Jang worked. High ranking officers were allowed to have an apartment in the officers' quarters because of the nature of their job. It was believed that providing senior officers with accommodation in the officers' quarters would assist in ensuring the security of high-ranking officers and their families and also would enable senior officers to get to the police station quickly enough should they be needed.

Mr Jang chose not to have his family move in with him into the officers' quarters, but instead decided to let them stay at their custom-built home – a massive and a very beautiful six-bedroom property in the mainland area of Lagos State. He usually went home to his family, save for occasions when Aunty Esther came and stayed the night with him. Mrs Jang is a very reliable, devoted and unsuspecting wife. She never questioned the integrity of her husband. Or maybe Mrs Jang chose to ignore the suspicion, like most other women who have an inkling that their husbands might be having an extra-marital affair but chose to turn a blind eye to it.

It was common practice in Lagos for a husband to have a mistress on the side. There was no problem as long as it was kept outside the family home and was not allowed to affect the person's home life.

"Where is Roger?" Mr Jang asked. (Roger was Mr Jang's allocated driver).

"He's here with me"

"Which car did you take?"

"The official car of course. You told us to take the official car." The official car was an unmarked vehicle belonging to the Nigerian Police Force which was assigned to senior police officers for official use. It was true Mr Jang had told Roger to use the official car to drive Aunty Esther home, in order not to be found out in case Mrs Jang saw another woman in their family car. As Roger was still on duty, he was wearing his police uniform.

"But what are you doing on the bridge?" asked Mr Jang. "You were supposed to be going home. Let me talk to Roger." Roger was put on the line. "What are you doing on the bridge. I told you to take her home?"

"Madam say she no wan go home sir. She wan me drop her at her friend's house sir," Roger replied. Mr Jang sighed heavily.

"Have you got any ammunition on you?"

"No sir," replied Roger.

"Good. Stay low and don't do anything stupid. I'll think about what to do. Don't do anything stupid. Okay? Put the phone on silent because I might ring you later."

Mr Jang knew there was a problem. He might find himself in trouble. The car was not expected to be on the bridge at that particular time and should anything happen to the official car, he might find it difficult to justify why it was on the bridge. He might also get into trouble with Mrs Jang, should it be found out that her husband had been having an extra-marital affair. Mr Jang immediately called an emergency meeting.

"There is a hold-up by armed robbers on the bridge. It is our duty to uphold the law."

"But sir, we haven't got weapons".

"Yeah, we'll use whatever we've got. Remember we are defending the law and they are on the wrong side of the law." All the junior officers looked at each other but they had no say in it. They had to obey their superior.

"Yes sir," they all replied.

Mr Jang suggested that they prepare two police vehicles full of armed police officers. Looking at the faces of many of the junior officers, one could see the look of resignation on their faces. This was one of the things they had been employed to do but they knew it could also be their last assignment. Many were valiant officers willing and ready to serve their community but they were poorly remunerated and a lack of adequate resources had demoralized many of them. However, duty was calling and they had to obey.

"Make sure that your guns are working properly."

Each officer took a brief look at the guns they were carrying as if they were praying silently and hoping that they worked. The guns were old and there was no record of them having had regular checks or services

"Please, don't drive too close to the bridge. We must assess the situation first before taking up our position," said Superintendent Jang. It was necessary for him to give them instructions then, and to make himself clear, as there was no two-way radio facility available to give instructions on once the operation got under way.

CHAPTER **3**

Meanwhile on the bridge, the armed robbery continued uninterrupted. The robbers must have gone through not more than ten vehicles, when all of a sudden, the sounds of gun shots were heard that definitely had not come from the robbers. That startled the robbers.

On hearing the gun shots which sounded like they were a fair distance from where the other members of the group were, Ade and Ben who had been standing by the vehicles, looked in the direction that the sound of gun shots had come from, and then stared at each other. John, one of the armed robbers' drivers quickly got out of the car he was in. He looked further towards one of the raiding group members and confirmed that the gunshots were not from his co-robbers. The look on his face told it all – as he realised there was trouble!

Realizing that the gun shots had not come from his co-robbers, John slowly approached Mike – the other driver of the car belonging to the armed robbers and signalled Mike to come down. Mike had heard the gun shots but wasn't sure whether or not they were from the other gang members.

John was an army officer. He has had wartime experience as he had once been posted to serve as part of a UN mission to the civil war in Somalia. He was married with two children. He was discharged from the army having sustained a life-changing injury in a UN operation in Somalia. His right leg was amputated below the knee and he was given a prosthetic leg. On his return from Somalia and after his treatment, he was discharged from the army but had to wait for his gratuity payment. As a matter of fact, it took over two years before the payment was processed. Every time he attended the military office where the payment was being processed, he would be told there were issues delaying the processing and was told to return at another time. During this period, the family relied on his wife's meagre irregular income. She worked at a private firm and sometimes her salary was not paid. There was little she could do, as there were no labour laws to protect her from this kind of practice. Even employees of the government sometimes suffered similar treatment.

After about two years of waiting, he was eventually approached by one of the workers at the section where the gratuity was being processed and it was explained to him why it had taken so long for his gratuity to be processed. They required him to pay a bribe or at least agree to share the gratuity. If he agreed, then his gratuity would be processed quickly and he would get his payment. John was told that the going rate was fifty percent of his gratuity. At first, he had felt that this was too much and he refused to cooperate. He managed to complain to one of the senior officers at the department and was promised an investigation. However, he soon realized that nothing would be done, as this was the way the game was played. If you wanted payment, you had to negotiate and be prepared to part with some of your gratuity. Realizing that he was banging his head against a brick wall, he finally agreed and within days, his gratuity was processed and he received half of his entitlement, even though he had to sign a document saying that he had received the full amount.

With his gratuity finally paid, John tried his hand at various types of business undertakings but failed. First, he used the money to buy a minibus and tried running a transport business. He hired a driver to drive the bus and to deliver a certain agreed amount to John every day. The agreed amount was only delivered in the first week. After that, there was always an excuse saying why the agreed amount could not be met. The reasons for that ranged from technical problem with the engine and having to pay the mechanic to carry out repairs, to being stopped by the police and having to part with a substantial amount of the day's revenue in bribes. John knew the former reason was not unusual, even though the vehicle was registered as a commercial transport vehicle, and all the necessary documents had been obtained and all the requirements were complied with.

There were days when no money was delivered at all. Eventually, John became frustrated and sold the vehicle. He tried his hand at importing goods from neighbouring countries to sell at a profit back home. He became frustrated by the amounts he had to pay in bribes to the customs officers at the border, which ate deep into his profit margin, even though what he was doing was not illegal. The death knell of his importing business came one day when he refused to pay the bribe he was asked for.

He said to himself that he couldn't continue like that, and he was prepared to go all the way to fight what he believed was an injustice. However, the custom officers were determined to make an example of him and seized his goods. He was then arrested and taken to the customs building not far from the border. At the customs building, he was made to wait for a very long time before being called to the desk. The officer at the desk brought out the report book and asked him questions about his name and why he had been arrested and brought into the building. John explained himself very clearly and asked the officer at the desk why he had been arrested in the first place. The officer explained to him that he was believed to be importing contraband goods into the country. John replied that that must have been a mistake as he had all the documentation for his goods which he showed to the officer.

The officer looked through the documents and asked John to go back to where he was sitting and said he would call him after he had checked whether the documentation was genuine. After a few hours had passed and no one had called him, John got up from where he was sitting and went to the desk. The officer apologized to him and explained to him that the reason why he had not been called back to the desk was because they couldn't get through to the department dealing with verification and he had left a message for the department to get back to them at the customs building. It was getting towards closing time and John was still waiting. He then went to the officer at the desk to ask what was going to happen. John was told to return the following day.

He asked for his paperwork, and it was given back to him after copies had been made. The following day, John returned but was told the same story as the day before. John kept returning and was given the same explanation every day until one day when he met one of the senior officers who frankly explained to him that the issue was not whether what he was doing was right or wrong, legal or illegal; but rather because he was expected to pay the bribe as a rite of passage, because the junior officers stationed at the border were expected by the senior officers who posted them there, to deliver a certain amount every day to share with the senior officers as a thank you for posting them to the border. Posting to the border is considered lucrative for any customs officer and only the favoured few got such postings. They were expected to say thank you in kind, for the opportunity, as it allowed them to make extra money on top of their meagre salary, which sometimes was not paid on time. Therefore, trying to fight against the officers who arrested him was like fighting the whole institution of the Nigerian Customs.

John was even told that due to his effort in fighting for justice, he would then have to pay more money because coming to the station meant that his case had now become bigger than if it had been settled at the border. Eventually, John was asked to pay an amount that was far bigger than he would have paid in bribes at the border. He did not have enough money on him or in his savings to meet the amount being asked for due to the increased bribe. Meanwhile, his merchandise was being kept at the depot and he was not allowed to reclaim it until he had made the payment. Throughout the time his merchandise was kept at the depot, John was not able to sell his merchandise; and with no other source of income to provide for his family, he found himself in debt. That meant that by the time he found out what he had to do to recover his merchandise, John had to borrow money to feed himself and his family and meet all his other expenses.

John tried to negotiate with the custom officers to at least reduce the amount they were asking for but they would not budge. Eventually, John went round his friends and relatives asking for help, in order to raise the amount that was demanded. After he had raised sufficient funds, he returned to the custom depot and made payment. It was only then that his merchandise was released to him. On returning home and checking his merchandise, he noticed that a substantial amount of the merchandise was missing but there was no one to complain to; no one to help him to obtain justice, even though he had done nothing wrong. He had to suffer the loss and the injustice in silence.

The final straw came one day when his street was targeted by a gang of armed robbers. They were going from house to house unhindered and robbing the residents of their valuables. The armed robbers even came with a large lorry to cart away the loot. Before the armed robbers got to his house, he heard the sounds of gunshots, he looked out through the window and saw some of the armed robbers carrying automatic weapons. He reached for his mobile phone and rang the nearest police station to report what was going on. He managed to describe the area and to give his address to the police and reported to the police fully what was going on. The officer at the other end of the phone promised him that they would send officers around soon. He had hoped that before the armed robbers got to his apartment, the police would have arrived and put a stop to the robbery. Instead, what happened was that after almost thirty minutes, the armed robbers got to his apartment.

However, to his disappointment, the police only arrived on his street hours after the armed robbers had completed their mission and left. By then, they had got to his apartment, ransacked his home and left with all his valuables, including his merchandise. He was kicked on the left eye when he tried to prevent one of the armed robbers from raping his thirteen-year-old daughter. It was a very bad experience for him and his family that night. The robbers were never caught; his belongings were never recovered, and neither was there any support for him and his family; and particularly, his daughter to deal with the emotional trauma of what they had experienced at the hands of the robbers. Afterwards, John was left destitute and had to look for other ways to sustain himself and his family.

Mike although he had been with the gang for quite some time now, had never experienced anything like this. Mike, unlike John had always had it rough. He was born and brought up in Lagos. He was the seventh of ten children borne by his mother to his absent father. It was reported that his father – an illiterate, was a well-known rascal who engaged in fraud and duping people. He would borrow money but never pay it back. He would collect money from neighbours promising to sell them goods, but never delivered the goods or returned the money, and if anyone confronted him, he would fight the person. He had spent times in prison for various offences, ranging from common assault to attempted murder. None of Mike's siblings ever studied beyond secondary school education. Their mother a petty trader was the only parent trying to provide for the children, but with her little income, the children knew that they have to fend for themselves as there was never enough to cater for all of them or provide for their needs. The children including Mike, learnt at an early age to fend for themselves.

Mike like the rest of his siblings, managed to complete his primary and secondary school education but that was how far as it went for Mike in education. He never pursued higher education. Even during his secondary school days, at the weekends, he had to hawk goods to make some money. Whenever, he failed to make enough money to last him till the next weekend, he added to it by stealing and extorting money from other hapless young people, who were physically weaker than him. When he completed his secondary school education and with no hope of a good job, Mike started to roam the streets and smoke weed. From that, Mike graduated to robbery – breaking into cars and snatching bags and valuables including jewellery from people on the street. He soon got mixed up with a group of youngsters in his locality who introduced him to stealing cars and selling them. He also became an errand boy for the senior boys on the street and was later introduced to hard drugs. He started to push drugs and travelled abroad with hard drugs concealed in his stomach. He was later caught and spent years in prison in the USA, before being deported back to Nigeria after he completed his sentence.

His face was among the faces published in one of the national newspapers when the government decided to name and shame Nigerians spending time in prison abroad for drug trafficking. As his face had become known all over the world, he felt it would be a big risk to continue with drug trafficking, and he decided to get involved in other illegal activities instead. He met Small Boy on the street who introduced him to the group. Due to his experience and expertise in breaking into cars and driving stolen vehicles; combined with his good knowledge of the Lagos metropolis, he became the driver for the group. He would steal a vehicle the group needed for its operation and would then drive the group to and from their destinations. There was no national database of vehicles there. This made it easier for someone like Mike to steal vehicles and move the vehicles around the country without being caught. Mike did not see himself as anything other than a career criminal. That was the only way he knew to survive. His parents and some of his siblings knew what he was getting involved with, but no one bothered to dissuade him from it.

Meanwhile, the other robbers among the raiding parties looked in the direction where the gun shot sounds appeared to have come from and noticed police vehicles with police officers jumping out and taking their positions around the bridge.

"Imam!" Small Boy said to one of his co-robbers. "The police are here."

"What! It can't be. They don't disturb us, we don't disturb them," replied Imam.

"It is the police," said Adio who was standing beside Small Boy.

Imam looked to where Small Boy was pointing, and saw police officers jumping out of their vehicles and taking up their positions. All the robbers retreated to where their vehicles were and took-up positions to defend their loot.

"What! There must be something wrong today. This is not real," said the Chief to another member of the gang who was with the other group that was heading north before the police arrived.

"What's the matter with them? Are they trying to commit collective suicide or what? They know we're better armed than they are; so, what are they trying to do?" said Priest, another member of the group of armed robbers.

"Well … we need to return fire for fire," said Small Boy, as the two groups of armed robbers came together and took cover from the incoming fire from the police.

"You know, this has never happened to me before. The police don't cross my path and I don't cross theirs," said Priest.

"Well, it's happening now," said Adio.

"Hmm," sighed Bobby, the de facto leader of the whole gang of armed robbers. He knew there was serious trouble whenever the police decided to confront armed robbers.

CHAPTER **4**

Among ordinary people caught up on the bridge on this fateful day were Mr Isaac and his pregnant wife. They had been married for over ten years and this was their first child. Early in the morning, Janet his wife started to feel uncomfortable. She was heavily pregnant but she was not due until the following month. They were not sure whether it was the onset of labour or just one of the discomforts of pregnancy. The couple decided to go for a check-up with their private doctor at a private clinic. Mr Isaac decided to take her there himself. Another more important reason why Mr Isaac decided to go with his wife was that, during the past four generations in his family, the firstborn children had never been able to know the father. It happened when he was born. His father died shortly before he was born. He was told that similar things had happened to his grandfather, his great grandfather and his great-great grandfather.

The death of Mr Isaac's father was a result of a freak accident. Old Mrs Isaac was heavily pregnant and on the fateful day, old Mr Isaac returned home from work and decided to have a lie down before having his dinner. A few moments later, he had his dinner and sat down relaxing on the sofa in the sitting room. His wife then told him that they had run out of bread and that she would need bread to prepare his breakfast the following morning. Old Mr Isaac quickly took some money and walked out of the house to go and buy some bread. The shop where they sold the bread was a short walk away, a few metres from their house. Shortly after he left the house, a dark cloud gathered in the sky and it looked as if it was going to rain. Because the shop where he was going to buy the bread was not far, he ignored the cloudy sky and quickly left. The rain started and became heavy. Just as he was about to step into his house with the bread in his hand, there was a sound of thunder and lightning. He fell to the floor and smoke started to come out of his head. He had been struck by lightning. All efforts to revive him failed. He was pronounced dead at the scene. A few days later, old Mrs Isaac gave birth to the current Mr Isaac.

It was a similar story with Mr Isaac's grandfather. The grandfather was involved in a road accident when his wife was due to have their first baby. He was travelling in public transport with a friend sitting beside him. Their vehicle reached a junction and had stopped for a traffic light. Just as the traffic light changed, signalling for their vehicle to go, there was another vehicle that was supposed to stop but was trying to beat the traffic light. It drove into the side of the vehicle in which Mr Isaac's grandfather and his friend were travelling; crashing into their vehicle at the exact spot where Mr Isaac's grandfather was sitting. Some other passengers were slightly injured, including the friend who was travelling in the same vehicle with Mr Isaac's grandfather, but Mr Isaac's grandfather was badly injured. He died shortly afterwards on the way to the hospital. His wife gave birth the following day.

A similar fate had befallen Mr Isaac's great grandfather. He also died few weeks before Mr Isaac's great grandmother gave birth to their first born. The husband had decided to travel to their village to visit his mother who had been ill for some time. He did not take his wife with him for the journey, as she was heavily pregnant. He got there safely and spent a few hours with his mother. When he was walking back to his car, he was bitten by a snake. They tried to get him to the nearest hospital which was a few miles away, but he died on the way to the hospital. His wife gave birth few weeks after that.

Mr Isaac was aware of all these stories and was determined to break what to him was a generational curse. Legend had it that someone had placed a curse on one of Mr Isaac's ancestors and the curse had stuck to the family ever since; affecting succeeding generations of Mr Isaac's line.

The story went thus: Once upon a time, there was a very great famine in the land where Mr Isaac's ancestors lived. The family's trade was farming but when the famine became very severe, one of Mr Isaac's ancestors, a very shrewd man called Dare decided to change his trade and went into travelling buying and importing goods from different countries, along the coast of West Africa. Sometimes he would go away for weeks and on his return, he brought back merchandise that he sold to the locals for a profit. There was a story that while he was travelling to another country in West Africa, he got to meet many people from Nigeria who had relocated to the West African country. He got to meet them often on his travels and a type of trust developed between him and them. A particular man happened to know Dare very well, as he had come from the same village that Dare had come from. The man left behind in the village, his old mother and the wife he had just married not long before the famine began. Every time Dare travelled to that particular country, he made it a point of duty to see the man from his village and bring him news about the welfare of his family.

After some time, the man felt it was much cheaper to send money and goods through Dare rather than through the bank or courier service. Dare was expected to deliver the money and goods to the man's family and bring back news about their wellbeing. As the man was doing very well in his new country of abode, he felt it was better for him to buy land in his local village back home in Nigeria and build a home for himself and his family. He discussed his plan with Dare who expressed his approval and promised to help the man in any way he could. The man would therefore send money regularly through Dare in the hope that Dare would assist in delivering the goods to his family back in their village and use the money for the purpose it was meant for. At first, the man gave Dare some money to help him buy a plot of land in the village and soon afterwards, he regularly gave money to Dare that he could use to build a home on the land. Dare would take the money and bring back updates about the project with pictures. After so many years; and in particular when Dare brought back news of the completion of the project, the man decided it was time to go back home and retire to his newly built house in Nigeria and enjoy the rest of his life with his family and in particular his young wife and son, who he had not seen for a very long time.

On returning home, he discovered that not only had Dare not used the money for the project it was meant for but he had stopped delivering the goods sent by the man for his family. The man's old mother had died of hunger and his young wife had remarried after failing to hear from him for a very long time. In his anger, the man cursed Dare saying, "For what you did, your lineage will never survive." Since then, every male born in Dare's line had never lived to see his first born.

The current Mr Isaac and his wife had a beautiful wedding attended by family members and well-wishers, but the wife failed to conceive. They were a very devoted Christian couple. They attended their local church regularly and prayed fervently. The couple tried every means they knew to have a child, including medical assistance, but all proved unsuccessful. Seeing all their efforts not yielding any positive result, the couple decided to just let nature take its course and concentrated their efforts on making sure that they enjoyed their lives together. Their tenth wedding anniversary came and they celebrated it with family members and close friends. About four months later, Mrs Isaac woke up one morning complaining of being ill. The couple at first didn't take the illness seriously, thinking that she would soon get better. However, by the following morning Mrs Isaac's condition rather than getting better had become worse. Mr Isaac decided to take his wife to see their private doctor for diagnosis and treatment; only to be told that she was two months pregnant. That took them by surprise as they had more or less given up on having their own child. They were nevertheless very happy.

Since the news about the pregnancy, Mr Isaac had asked his wife to stop working to make sure the pregnancy was not endangered in any way. With his knowledge of the history in the family, he realized that the death of the husband always occurs close to the time of the delivery of the first and only child but nothing happens to the mother and the baby. As the estimated delivery date of their first child was approaching, Mr Isaac became alert and very conscious of what he did, where he went and what risks he was prepared to take. He therefore decided that he would make sure that he and his heavily pregnant wife would always be together, believing that in this way he would be safe. He was not expecting to get caught up in an armed robbery and particularly not on the bridge that he had frequently travelled on an uncountable number of times. Something like this only happens to some other people, so it seems. As a matter of fact, when the robbers called on him and his wife in their car and seeing that the woman was heavily pregnant and appeared to be in some discomfort, the robbers decided not to take anything from them and did not bother them. Mr Isaac was also very cooperative and very compliant with the armed robbers and the robbers didn't spend much time with them. Adio took pity on them and called on the others to leave them alone. However, the anxiety of the whole situation appeared to have gotten to Mrs Isaac and might have brought-on the full early signs of labour. Mr Isaac and his wife were now caught up in the middle of an exchange of gunfire between the police and the gang of armed robbers.

Meanwhile, the police took their position under the command of Superintendent Jang. They all ducked as gun shots started coming in from the robbers' position. They too returned fire. Superintendent Jang used his binoculars to locate the position of the robbers. He then asked two of his officers to try and move forward towards the robbers, while the other officers continue to shoot to provide cover. John, one of the robbers sensed that something was happening. He knew from his experience in the army that usually, when there was continuous incoming fire without a specific target, it was always to provide cover. He quickly moved away from the rest of the gang. He looked under the vehicles and saw the boots of the advancing police officers. He was able to identify the location of the advancing police officers. He grabbed one of the hand grenades, removed the pin and threw it into the midst of the advancing officers. As soon as the grenade exploded, he rose up from his position and opened fire. The officers were hit as they tried to avoid the hand grenade and died instantly from their wounds. Now that the lives of police officers had been taken, the police had to see the matter through to the bitter end; and in this kind of situation, the bitter end is always for the law breakers. The upholder of the law always triumphed even when much had to be sacrificed. The robbers knew that the police would be incensed by these deaths. There was no holding back now. This was it! Superintendent Jang saw the deaths. No matter how inferior their ammunitions were, they were the ones fighting on the side of the law and they could not be seen as having been defeated. He asked for more officers to open fire. One of the armed robbers, John was hit and seriously wounded. The others had no time to attend to him as more shots were coming in from the police side. He later died from the gunshot wound he sustained. Still there was no let up from the fire coming from the police.

Another armed robber, Mike was hit and killed. The rest of the gang were doing their best to continue the fight. The police officers seemed to have advanced from their position as the fire coming from them seemed to be more frequent than before. Priest got hold of another hand grenade, activated it and threw it towards the police while the others also opened fire on the police. Another officer was badly injured and this appeared to have incensed the police even more and they increased their firing at the robbers. Another robber, Ben was hit in the shoulder. One of the robbers tore off part of the shirt Ben was wearing and tied it around the wound to stem the loss of blood. Ben took his gun in his other hand and continued to shoot. He was doing his best to carry on the fight.

Ben was not one who gave up easily although he had only joined the group only recently. His parents had moved to Lagos a long time ago, before Ben was born. Ben was born and brought up in Lagos. As far as his family was concerned, Ben was an aberration. His father was a medical doctor and his mother a successful bank manager. Ben had two siblings – a brother and a sister who were successful in their own right. Ben was the youngest of the three children. Right from his younger days, he had shown himself to be different from his family. He was often in trouble at school and he had been suspended from school many times, for one reason or another. After primary education, his parents decided to send him to a boarding school away from Lagos in the hope that it would help to get him onto a straighter path. This only lasted for two years as he was expelled for stealing exam papers prior to the exams.

At the age of thirteen, his parents decided to send him to live with his uncle in the UK thinking a change of environment would help him. However, that only lasted five years as he often got into trouble with the law and was always at the revolving door of the juvenile courts in England. After another brush with the law in which he was accused of being part of a group of four young boys who gang-raped a thirteen year old girl, his uncle felt he had had enough. Ben did not rape the girl himself but was accused of setting the crime in motion, as he was the person who called out to the girl as she was walking home from school and as soon as she stopped to see who was calling her, the other three pounced on her and raped her, taking turns doing so. Ben just stood there watching. He did not try to rescue the girl or call for help. At the trial and due to his past criminal history, he was given a custodial sentence. After his release from a youth detention centre, he was sent back to his parents in Nigeria.

On his return to Nigeria, Ben's parents tried to get him to learn one trade or another, but every attempt failed. He continued getting himself into trouble and often his father had to go to the police station to bail him out. At a certain point, his father stopped answering his phone calls as he would call his parents whenever he was arrested by the police. He shifted his calls to his mother and after many appearances at various police stations, she too got fed up and stopped taking his calls. Eventually, Ben's parents appeared to give up on him.

There was one incident when after his arrest, the police rang the mother to inform her of what has happened and where her son was and asked whether she would like to come down to the police station to post bail for him; and his mother famously replied, "I thought you had called to inform me that he was dead. Please only call me when he dies, and we will come and recover his body." The message was passed onto Ben that his mother had refused to come down to see him and he was also told that he was not welcome back in the family home. Ben then started to roam the streets of Lagos. That was where he met men like himself who introduced him to various vices and eventually to armed robbery.

Meanwhile, Ben continued to lose blood from his wound and started to get weaker and weaker. He raised his gun once more and fired a shot before lowering the gun as he was too weak to lift the gun. He eventually died.

Knowing that the robbers had hand grenades with them, Superintendent Jang decided that it might not be a good idea to move any closer and he asked the officers to withdraw a little bit further away, so as to be out of the range of the hand grenades.

The exchange of fire from both sides continued intermittently. Another robber Adio got hit by incoming fire and was badly injured. There was little they could do for him. He soon bled to death. The death of Adio might have had a profound impact on the rest of the group. They knew his story and for him to meet such an end, was brutal they thought.

Adio was a young man from the western part of Nigeria. He had graduated a few years earlier with a BSc (hons) degree in

Economics from his home state university. His original intention was to further his studies to doctorate level but due to incessant strikes by university lecturers and frequent closure of the universities he attended, the degree course which should have lasted no more than four years had lasted six years.

Adio came from a large family – two brothers and five sisters. He was the first born. His parents had hoped that he would complete his education on time, find a job and assist in the funding of the education of his younger siblings. Adio had wanted to study for a post-graduate professional course to improve his employability and to command a good salary but the fact that his university course had taken longer to complete meant that his immediate sibling had also gained entry into a university just as he was completing his and his family could not afford to pay for two university students at the same time. It was decided that Adio should look for a job to sustain himself while the parents supported and funded his sister through her university course. Adio with his determination to further his education, decided to go into farming to fund his post-graduate education which he did with no support from his parents.

After completing his Master's degree, he went into teaching and got a job at a secondary school close to his home town. However, he got disillusioned with the profession as there were incessant strikes due to poor remuneration in the profession and the teachers trying to secure improved working conditions for themselves. He had watched the situation in the teaching profession gradually becoming worse. He later decided to move to Lagos for a better life. His decision to migrate to Lagos was influenced by the fact that teachers' pay in the countryside was not very good, compared to the cities and there had been times when salary payments had been delayed resulting in many teachers getting into debt. He had thought that things would be much better in Lagos and at least the pay would be better than it was in his home state. Adio was right about the pay which was better in Lagos but he was wrong about the other issues. Payment of teachers' salaries was not regular and there were times when salary payments had been delayed for months. The irregularity of the payments meant that he was always in debt as other costs of living had to be met. The cost of living in Lagos is also higher compared to the outer regions.

There was one strike action that Adio would always remember. He found a job at a high school and things were going well for him. However, a few months into his employment there was a long delay in the payment of teachers' salaries in the state and the Teachers' Union decided to go on strike. The strike lasted well over six months. The teachers had therefore not received any salary for over six months. With or without strikes, workers pay sometimes went unpaid for several months anyway, and they either had to borrow money to bridge the gap or do other trades beside their teaching profession, to supplement their salaries. Some teachers were known to have resorted to making sandwiches to bring to school to sell to the students, in order to make ends meet.

After a long-time persevering, Adio felt he could not continue in the same way and he decided to leave the profession to run a business of buying and reselling luxurious goods like expensive wrist watches, gold and trinkets. In Lagos, Adio had met a lady, Beatrice at a job interview he had attended. Beatrice was there for an interview for the same post. They struck up a conversation and ended up exchanging numbers. They became good friends and from her, Adio found out much about life in Lagos. He discovered how difficult living in Lagos could be, and about the problems facing university graduates trying to find a job. Adio's friendship with Beatrice developed into a relationship and Adio became very close to Beatrice's family. He was later introduced to one of Beatrice's brothers who happened to be Bobby.

At first, Adio's relationship with Beatrice was very useful in boosting his business as he was introduced to many clients. However, there came a prolonged period of downturn in his business and

Adio tried to find out about life in the Nigerian Police Force, hoping that Bobby would help him to get into Nigeria's Police Force. When Adio saw the financial struggle Bobby faced, despite his employment with the police force, he started to have second thoughts. Bobby's dismissal from the police force put paid to any lingering thought of Adio going into the police force. In his desperation to find a job, Adio thought about returning to the teaching profession, but he soon discovered how difficult that could be, particularly if you have no one to assist you with securing the job; preferably someone with influence who would use his or her position to secure the job for you. There were too many jobless graduates chasing posts. It was not about how qualified you were or how good you were but rather about who you knew. In his effort to secure a livelihood for himself and his young family, Adio started to go for jobs that came his way including temporary and even poorly-paid jobs. Eventually, Adio married Beatrice and after their first child and still with no regular job, the young family started to have financial difficulties. There were times when Adio would have no job at all and Bobby would provide financial assistance to the couple. In his sympathy for his sister and her husband, Bobby decided to introduce Adio to the illegal world and eventually to the group. Since then, Adio and his young family had been financially well provided for.

After the death of Adio, there was an eerie silence among the remaining armed robbers, particularly Bobby, who was then saddled with the unenvied position of having to explain to his sister what happened to her husband. However, he first had to negotiate his escape from the bridge first, or at least survive what they saw as an ambush by the police.

"What are you going to tell your sister?" asked Priest. The other members of the group knew how Bobby and Adio were related. Bobby sighed heavily in response.

"I don't want to be paraded in front of any stupid press," said Priest.

"Neither do I," said Chief.

Small Boy – the youngest of the group stared long and hard at the ground. This was not what he had expected when he joined the group. He had hoped to live a longer life and start a family of his own; get married and have children, and one day quit the life of crime; but all his dreams seemed to be crashing down, suddenly. How would his family and, in particular his mum took the news of him being caught as a member of a team of armed robbers? What about the trial and the sentencing, of being paraded in front of the press and the shame he would bring to his mother? What about the neighbours who had seen him dressing well and going out; thinking he was working and doing well in life. All his secrets would be exposed to the world. Many of these thoughts started going through Small Boy's mind.

CHAPTER **5**

Mrs Isaac meanwhile went into premature labour. Mr Isaac panicked and shouted, "Help!" The sound of gunshots must have drowned his call for help, as no one heeded his call but the firing and returning of fire continued. Mr Isaac in his nervous state, opened the door of his car and shouted very loudly, "Please help!" The loudness of his voice must have startled and confused the robbers and the police so much that gunshots went astray and one or two appeared to have gone in the direction of the car where Mr and Mrs Isaac were. This was followed by total quiet on the bridge, to the extent that his follow up call for help could be heard from far away, even though it wasn't as loud as the earlier shout for help. As Mr Isaac's car was closer to the armed robbers than to the police, he knew that it was going to be difficult but he hoped against hope that the robbers who had shown him and his wife compassion earlier-on would still be sympathetic and show them compassion again.

"Please help. We need a doctor." Out of concern and willingness to help, a doctor who was also held up on the bridge shouted back. "I am a doctor" directly at the robbers. Priest who had been firing at the police signalled to the doctor to go towards the couple and help if he could. The doctor crouching, slowly moved towards the car where Mr and Mrs Isaac were. The doctor, on moving closer saw Mrs Isaac sitting at the back of the car sweating and clearly seeming to be in an advanced stage of labour. Mr Isaac, sitting on the floor, close to the car, with his right hand on the left side of his chest slowly beckoned the doctor towards his wife with his head. The doctor noticed the bloodstain on Mr Isaac's clothes.

"What happened?" the doctor asked.

"My wife … my wife … She … is … in labour," Mr Isaac stammered; which indicated that he too was in serious pain.

"But what happened to you?" the doctor asked

"My… my wife first," Mr Isaac replied. The doctor was confused. He didn't know who he should attend to first. Mr Isaac noticed this and pointed towards his wife. The doctor moved closer to Mrs Isaac and noticed that she had started to push as the baby had started to come out. The doctor helped her deliver the baby. "It's a girl " said the doctor as he placed the baby into Mrs Isaac's hands.

"She's beautiful" said Mr Isaac as he reached out his hands with great difficulty towards his wife almost knocking the baby off from her hands. He had been hit by a stray bullet. They weren't sure where the bullet came from – whether from the robbers or from the police. It appeared that one of the bullets had hit Mr Isaac in the chest.

"Help doctor!" Mrs Isaac said. "Hold on honey, you'll be fine."

The doctor helped Mr Isaac to sit up, with his back leaning against the car. The doctor checked Mr Isaac's wound. He realised that Mr Isaac had lost a great deal of blood and there was little he could do to help as the firing had started once again. Mr Isaac leaned towards his wife and the baby. He stared at the baby and then at his wife.

"She … she's beautiful," he said, trying to smile.

"Hold on honey, you'll be fine," Mrs Isaac said, noticing that her husband was in serious pain. Mr Isaac tried to take a long, big breath as if he were struggling to breathe.

"You're beautiful," Mr Isaac said to his wife.

He appeared to be going in and out of consciousness. He looked at the baby again and beckoned the doctor to put the baby in his arms. The doctor took the baby from Mrs Isaac and put the baby in Mr Isaac's arms.

"She … she's … beautiful," Mr Isaac said, slurring his words as he stared at the baby. "We … we … did it! We … we … did it. We broke the curse," he said.

"Hold on honey, you'll be fine," Mrs Isaac said to her husband.

"We did it," repeated Mr Isaac as he tried to smile at his wife. Mrs Isaac started to cry. "No … no … don't cry. Save it for me. Dear … save it … for me. It's a happy day … We did it. I love you … love you …," Mr Isaac said as he breathed his last. The doctor quickly took the baby from him. Mrs Isaac started to sob uncontrollably.

Meanwhile, the sounds of gunshots continued to be heard now and again from the positions of the robbers and the police.

"But I don't know why the police decided to cross our path. We never crossed theirs before and they never crossed ours," said Priest.

"Until today," added Chief. "If we had gone into one of those posh areas, I would have understood the police's involvement."

"But we didn't!" explained Imam.

"So, we don't go into areas where the rich people live?" asked Small Boy with a look of shock on his face.

"It wasn't like that," said Priest. "You see, to operate in the affluent areas carries more risk. Some of them have their own guns, their own security force, and the police are more likely to respond to their calls for help because of the big influence some of them have in the society, compared to the poor areas," explained Priest.

"So, we have been robbing the poor," said Small Boy. There was no reply from the other members of the group as everyone looked away.

"We have been robbing innocent, defenceless poor people. We are cowards," said Small Boy.

"Stop it. I am not a coward, I'm a professional," said Chief.

"We shot a woman back there. That could have been a member of my family. That could have been my mum. My family is poor. We are cowards," said Small Boy with tears rolling down his face.

"Keep quiet! I am not a coward!" shouted Chief.

Small Boy was a university graduate like Adio, He had a BSc in Economics, but since completing his university education ten years ago, he had failed to secure a permanent job. He was one of three children. His other siblings – a male and a female had died a few years before. The male died during a student protest against hiked school fees. It was a peaceful non-violent protest called by the National Student Union, but the government responded by sending heavily armed police officers to quell the protest. There was an accidental discharge of a bullet from a police officer's gun, which hit Small Boy's brother in the head. They tried to get him to hospital but he died on the way. There was no government operated ambulance in Lagos. You had to take your sick or injured people to the hospital yourself. The impact of the loss killed their father. His other sibling, a female, had died in the Mali Desert, trying to make her way into Europe. Small Boy witnessed the death.

It had been a very difficult life for Small Boy because after finishing his university education and being unable to secure a job, Small Boy decided to try his luck in Europe. The journey was treacherous. Africans trying to get into Europe without a visa would either seek the help of people smugglers or would hitch-hike their way to Morocco or Libya where at one of the ports they would pay people smugglers with a dinghy or ferry to get them across the Mediterranean Sea to Italy or Spain. You pay more for a ferry journey than for a dinghy. Whichever one you chose, it was still dangerous and many people had lost their lives trying to get to Europe that way. The ferry sometimes capsized and the inflated dinghies often deflated or burst; killing many or they drowned. Another difficult part of the journey was travelling through the Mali Desert. Many would-be travellers had come short in the desert. They succumbed to the treacherous conditions there. You could see their bones lying in the desert as you walked along.

The night before leaving Nigeria, Small Boy informed his sister of his intention to make the journey. He did not inform their mum. However, on getting to Mali, he was shocked to discover that his sister had also decided to make the journey through the desert.

"What are you doing here?" Small Boy asked his sister.

"I am fed up with the situation in Nigeria too. I need to leave and sort out my life abroad," was her reply.

"But this is too dangerous," said Small Boy.

"I know. That is the reason why I didn't tell you because you would try and dissuade me from going, but I will survive," replied his sister.

Small Boy tried as hard as he could to persuade his sister to return home, but it seemed that she had made up her mind. Small Boy decided that all he could do now was to help and protect his sister as much as possible as they travelled along together.

One day in the desert, as they were trekking along, they were picked up by patrolling Malian troops who threatened to shoot them unless they parted with their money. The Malian troops took some of their money and also raped Small Boy's sister. He witnessed the rape but there was little he could do to prevent it or protect his sister. The Malian officers were armed with guns. In her effort to prevent herself from getting pregnant, she decided to chew a plant she saw in the desert which she thought would be useful as it resembled a plant she had seen before when she was in Nigeria. She thought it might work to prevent any pregnancy because the plant was very bitter. However, she was wrong, the plant turned out to be poisonous. She died a few days afterwards. Small Boy buried her in the desert but never informed their mother. He thought the impact of the loss might be too much for their mother, considering that the family had already lost his brother and the thought and the grief of that loss resulted in the death of their father.

Eventually, Small Boy made it to Libya but by then, he had little money left and not enough to even pay one of the inflated prices the dinghy owners charged for the journey from the port in Libya to Europe. He hung around in Libya for a while. One day, he met another Nigerian who was also trying to make the journey across the sea to Europe. He offered to help Small Boy with some money to pay the dinghy owner. The agreement was that Small Boy would pay him back when they got to Europe. However, disaster struck not long into the sea journey – the dingy deflated and some of the occupants, including the Nigerian who had lent Small Boy the money drowned. Small Boy was fortunate enough to be picked up by a Libyan fishing boat. Those who were rescued that night were returned to Libya as they had not travelled far. He had no money left. After staying in Libya for a while, he decided to travel back to Nigeria. So, penniless, he hitch-hiked his way back.

With no money and no job, he decided to stay in Lagos, sleeping rough. There was no point in going back to the village now. There was no prospect of getting a job in the village and how could he face his mum and tell her the news of his sister's death? After the death of her husband, Small Boy's mum struggled to pay the school fees for Small Boy and his sister. By the time Small Boy finished his university education, his mum was heavily in debt. She was hoping that when Small Boy finished his university education, that he would be able to support the family and assist the mother financially. On finishing his university education, Small Boy tried but failed to secure any job in his home state. He then decided to travel to Lagos in search of a job but with no luck there either.

On his return from his ill-fated attempt to get to Europe through Libya, and while on the street in Lagos, Small Boy met Chief who after hearing his story, had compassion for him and introduced him to Priest and the rest of the group. Ever since he had been introduced to the group, Small Boy had been rolling in money. He sent money home to his mother regularly, but still kept the news of the death of his sister from their mother.

Meanwhile, on the bridge, Small Boy stared long and hard at the ground as tears continued to roll down his face. He put down the gun he was holding. The other members of the group turned their attention towards him. Small Boy then started to take off the bullet proof vest he was wearing. The group only had two bullet proof vests between them. One was given to Small Boy to protect him as he was the youngest among them. They drew lots for the other one. Priest was the lucky one who got the other bullet proof vest.

"What's he doing?" Chief asked, as Small Boy put the bullet proof vest on the floor after taking it off.

The other gang members looked on in amazement. Small Boy stood up and raised his arms up in a gesture of surrender and started to walk towards the police position. Chief cocked his gun as if he was going to shoot Small Boy. Priest stopped him pointing at Chief and shaking his head.

"Leave the boy alone, maybe he wants to make peace with his God before he dies," Priest said. In Nigeria, anyone caught involved in armed robbery is sentenced to death by firing squad – surrender or no surrender.

On the police side, one of the junior officers saw Small Boy with his hands raised walking towards them.

"Oga they are surrendering". The others looked in the direction of Small Boy.

"Only one of them," another officer said.

Superintendent Jang saw Small Boy with his hands raised in surrender. However, unsure whether or not the gang had noticed or had come across the official police car that was carrying his mistress, and afraid of what the surrendering gang member might say to the press if given the opportunity, Mr Jang decided to take steps to prevent his extra-marital affairs being exposed. Still fixating his eyes on the surrendering gang member, he ordered one of the junior officers to open fire.

"What! He is surrendering sir," the officer said.

"Open fire!" Superintendent Jang repeated sternly.

The officer opened fire and rained bullets on Small Boy. Small Boy was fatally wounded. The other gang members heard the gun shots and looked in the direction of Small Boy. Small Boy collapsed on his knees and muttered some words as he died.

He could be heard saying, "Mum was deprived even of her last surviving son."

The robbers realized that it was going to be a long fight and knowing that they were outnumbered by the police officers, they felt it was either a fight to the end or surrender.

"What a day this is! But didn't you consulted your Ifa Oracle before we embarked on this operation?" asked Imam, turning towards Chief.

"Yes I did," Chief replied.

"It seemed the Oracle failed us this time," said Priest.

"But you also prayed – to Allah, didn't you?" asked Chief, as he raised his head and looked straight at Imam.

"Everything failed us. Ifa, God, Allah, Everything!" said Imam.

"Well, it is written in the Bible that in the last days even prophesy will fail," said Priest. "Last days," retorted Imam with a wry smile. "This is our last day."

Today's operation was unlike any other the gang had undertaken before. They choose their targets very carefully. Prior to them embarking on any operation, the Chief would consult the Ifa Oracle, Imam would pray to Allah and the Priest would pray to God about it. If any of these three members objected to the operation, the group would not embark on it. That day's operation had received the tacit and express approval of everyone.

"Bastards! Why shoot a boy who was surrendering," said Chief. He picked up the bullet proof vest left behind by Small Boy and put it on. He then took in a big puff of the cigarette in his hand. He dropped the remaining cigarette and put the cigarette out by stamping on it with his foot. He brought out his mobile phone from his pocket and called his wife.

Chief a.k.a. Fadare hailed from the western part of Nigeria. He was a married man with two children – a five-year old boy and a fifteen month old girl. Chief was a university graduate with a Master's degree in urban studies. His wife whom he met while they were both studying at the university got a first class degree in political science. Chief came to Lagos a few years ago after completing his university studies with the hope of securing a permanent well paid job but things had not turned out as he would have liked. After many short-term temporary jobs, he decided to go into business selling car parts. He was assisted with the initial funding to start his business by his wife's family.

The business started off well and he made good money. He started by buying car parts from importers and selling them at retail prices. He was then introduced into travelling abroad to import second hand cars and this too started well until one day, all of a sudden and without any warning or notice the Nigerian government imposed a ban on cars that were over a certain age. He was badly hit by the ban, as he had already travelled abroad and made several purchases of cars he wanted to import and he had put them on the ship bound for Nigeria. He had to pay the customs extra money in backhand payments in order to clear his goods from the port, otherwise the vehicles would have been impounded as contraband. This ate deep into his profit and seriously affected his business. The showroom where he sold the cars was regularly raided by the police. The police must have been tipped off by the custom officials who had earlier allowed Chief to bring the vehicles in after he had bribed them at the port. The police therefore knew that the vehicles should not have been allowed into the country and he therefore became a soft target for them. Every time they raided his business, he had to pay them bribes to stop them from impounding his goods. Then finally disaster struck one evening. After close of business, a fire started in an adjoining building which resulted in the whole market complex being destroyed by fire.

Despite the emergency call to the fire brigade by those living nearby, it took some hours before the fire brigade arrived, and even after they arrived, they realized that their fire engine did not have enough water nor fire extinguishers to work with as the fire had spread by then. They tried to get water from a nearby public tap but discovered that there was no water flowing. That is a common occurrence in Nigeria. The cause of the fire was unknown but Chief's business was not insured. Many business-es are not insured here. It is not compulsory. Even those who are insured find it hard to get claims paid. His wife never had to work. The money from the business was more than enough to provide for the family. With a wife and two children to provide for, and with no other source of income, Chief joined the armed robbery gang. There is no social security in Lagos. You are on your own. It's survival of the fittest. Nigeria is where free and undiluted capitalism is practised.

"Honey! You never call me when you're at work. What hap-pened?" Chief was very open with his wife. She knew what her husband did to provide for his family.

"Small Boy is dead!" Chief told his wife.

"What! What happened?" his wife asked.

"The stupid police crossed us," Chief replied.

"Why? Don't they know you're better armed than they are?"

"Those bastards... I Just called to say I love you. Whatever happen, know that I love you and the kids so much."

"What's wrong! ... tell me," Chief's wife said in a shaky voice. Chief could imagine the fear and trepidation his wife was feeling.

"They're engaging us in a gun battle."

"What!" Chief's wife screamed. The noise from the scream might have woken up the couple's five-year old. Junior who had just woken up and still in his pyjamas walked towards his mother.

"What's wrong Mummy?" he asked, looking at his moth-er's face.

"It's Daddy," she replied.

"Is Daddy all right? Where is he ... let us go and get him." Chief heard the voice of his five-year old son in the background.

"Look after the kids. Remember, I love you all."

"It's Daddy," repeated Chief's wife as she put down the phone and tears started to roll down her face.

"Mummy, what's wrong with Daddy. Let's go and bring him home."

"No … we can't … we can't," she said, pulling her son closer to her sobbing uncontrollably.

Meanwhile, on the bridge, Chief lit another cigarette, took a large puff and threw it on the floor. He picked up his gun and stood up.

"Heaven here I come," he said and took a few steps forward and started to shoot in the direction of the police. He threw away all caution and continued to walk towards the police, shooting as he walked along.

"Bastards!" he shouted. "Bastards!" he repeated, as he continued shooting and walking towards the police. Some of his shots hit two police officers and one died immediately. One of the officers hit was Superintendent Jang. He was still alive. The other officers rained a barrage of shots on Chief and he slumped and died.

At the police line, the other officers immediately tried to arrange for Superintendent Jang to be taken to the nearest hospital. There was no spare police vehicle to take him and the government hospital did not operate an ambulance system. They had to wave down a taxi to rush him to the nearest hospital. He died on the way to the hospital.

When the other gang members saw that Chief was dead, they all stared eerily at the ground as if saying to themselves, "This is the end."

"I won't be captured alive," said Priest.

"Neither will I," said Imam.

Priest sighed heavily.

"This is it," said Bobby. He was the oldest member of the group and the de facto leader. He was very well respected within the group. He seldom talked but when he did, the rest of the group listened.

Bobby was a police officer. He had spent ten years in the Nigerian Police Force where he had been a sergeant until five years before, when he was dismissed for gross misconduct.

The inspector general of police in his effort to tackle corruption among police officers had issued a directive that no police officer could carry more than a certain amount of money on him or her, while on duty. This was because police officers had become notorious for taking bribes from people. The inspector general thought that by him issuing this directive, police officers would be dissuaded from taking bribes, knowing that being caught with an amount more than the specified amount would mean facing disciplinary action that might lead to a dismissal. Bobby was well aware of this new directive from the inspector general of police but; like many of his colleagues in the force, he thought he could avoid being caught.

However, one evening, just when he was about to finish his shift, a superintendent of police was driving by and noticed a police checkpoint operated by Bobby and four other officers. Bobby was the one holding the money collected in bribes that day. The superintendent noticed Bobby's bulging pocket and decided to investigate further. Bobby was asked to empty his pocket and was found to be carrying forty times more than the allowed amount for officers to carry. With no acceptable explanation as to how he came by the money, Bobby was dismissed from the force with immediate effect. With five children to provide for, Bobby starteded to get involved in illegal activities, including handling stolen goods, currency counterfeiting, impersonation and fraud. One day, he met Chief, one of the armed robbers, who introduced him to the rest of the gang. Since then, he had been involved in armed robbery. He had been a very valuable source of information to the group regarding the tactics used by the police and had also served as a link between the group and recalcitrant and wayward police officers who stole police weapons and sold them to the group. Consequently, Bobby became a very valuable member of the group and because of his age and experience in the Nigerian Police Force, he became the de facto leader of the group. His words and advice carried much weight within the group.

"So, what's next?" Bobby asked

"We just have to fight to the very end because I am not surrendering," answered Priest.

"You know when I was growing up and saw all the corruption in the country, I dreamt of becoming the president one day and purging the country of corruption," said Imam as he shook his head in despair.

"My parents wanted me to be a priest and do God's work, but I failed," explained Priest.

"I remember in high school we would talk among our friends about the corruption prevalent in our society. I hoped that one day I would join the army, become a senior officer and lead a revolution to sanitize the country," said Bobby.

"I dreamt of making a pilgrimage to Mecca – the Holy land and becoming an Alhaji – a clean and honest one, not like the ones we have today in our country," continued Imam.

"Many of them are rogues!" added Priest.

"They treat the idea of becoming Alhaji as a passport to obtaining government contracts. They visit the holy land and return, only to become more corrupt. They never help the poor and they deprive the citizens of their rights," said Bobby.

"They failed the country," said Priest.

"I failed too," said Ade. "I am a university graduate but what did I turn out to be? An area boy. There is nothing exciting about a forty-two year old being called an area boy," added Ade.

"I am not an area boy! I am a professional," protested Priest.

"But that is what we are – area boys," said Imam.

"No, I am not," repeated Priest.

"We are area boys. We are boys because we do not do what men do. We have no regular job," added Imam.

"This is my job," said Priest.

"What! Robbing people, murdering defenceless citizens and turning innocent children into orphans?" retorted Imam.

"What a contribution to human history," said Ade. "When you are as old as I am and have no regular job but hang around on the street, you are an area boy."

"We are area boys because we hang around in the area and we don't do what men do," explained Imam.

"But what else could I have done? It wasn't my fault. I was kicked out of the Convent. I managed to complete a university degree course but I couldn't find any other job," said Priest.

"So are many other Nigerians, in fact millions of them. It is no excuse to go about robbing others," said Bobby.

"This is my job. What is the difference? Our leaders are robbing the nation, we are robbing the people and in fact we are only robbing a small proportion of the people compared to our leaders. Our so-called leaders make even more money than we do, but no one accuses them or arrests them. They are robbing all the people … all the citizens," said Priest.

"Men! This land is a dream killer," said Bobby.

"No! Our leaders are. They turn what is supposed to be corporate blessings into individual wealth, to the exclusion of others," said Imam.

"Africa is a blessed continent, but the people are the most cursed," said Priest.

"That is down to our leaders," added Bobby.

"Look around. Out of all the continents in the world, Africa is the most blessed of them all," said Priest.

"But the people are suffering," added Bobby.

"Not our leaders, they are not suffering. They are enjoying," said Imam.

"If the Israelites are God's chosen people, we Africans are naturally God's own people," said Priest.

"Africa is the most blessed among the continents of the world. Look, this is a land where when you eat fruit and the seed falls on the ground, it grows by itself, you don't need to do much," said Imam.

"When there was famine in the time of Abraham, where did he go to escape the famine – Africa. When there was going to be severe famine in the world and God wanted to save the Israelites, where did he send them in order to save them from the famine – Africa," added Bobby.

"You are definitely right there," said Priest. "Even the Bible describes Africa as God's own garden… Genesis chapter 13 verse 10…," added Priest.

"Most the pity… Most the pity," said Imam repeatedly.

Just as they were finishing talking, another shot came in from the police ranks and hit Bobby in the head. He died instantly. The remaining members of the group stared at Bobby's lifeless body and shook their heads in despair.

Ade realized that his gun had run out of ammunition and he asked Priest for spares to reload. Priest passed on some spare ammunition to Ade but as he was reloading, he got hit in the neck by incoming fire. The remaining members of the group went to his aid and tried to stem the loss of blood. Imam took off the shirt Ade was wearing and put it on the spot where the bullet had hit Ade. The cloth soon became soaked in blood. Ade stared at his fellow members and shook his head as if admitting that his end is near.

This was a sad ending for Ade. Ade like Imam was into business. After completing his university education, he followed his father into the family business buying and selling goods. Sometimes he would travel abroad with his father to buy goods that they would bring back into the country to sell for a profit. Initially, business was going well and the family was doing well financially. After learning the trade from his father, Ade was helped by his father to set up on his own. His father paid for two years' rent for a shop not far from the family home and helped to stock the shop with various merchandise. Ade started off well and was making good money from the business. He got married and had four children. However, with success sometimes comes pride and various vices. Ade started to get involved with many women and started to drink and party heavily. He impregnated many women and took more wives, against the advice of his parents. Soon, his business started to fail and he then found himself in debt. Unable to meet the financial needs of his various wives and their children, he started to look for other means to supplement his income. He tried his hand at smuggling contraband goods and soon graduated into funding drug trafficking. Whilst he would not push the drugs himself, he hired men and women who trafficked the drugs for him and he funded their expenses and paid them for their work. One day, one of those working for him was arrested in Indonesia and was sentenced to death. After his execution, the man's family came and burnt down Ade's shop. They were looking for Ade to kill him to take revenge for the life of their son who had been executed. Ade had to run away and he settled in Lagos. There he met some friends who introduced him to armed robbery and he had been with the group ever since. He was hoping that one day he would stop doing armed robberies and return to his original business. Another gun shot came in and hit Ade on the chest. He died instantly.

More shots started to come in from the police. Another shot came hitting the car where the robbers were, narrowly missing Imam. The sound it made after hitting the car was very loud. Imam knew that he just had a very lucky escape.

Imam aka Abdul hailed from northern Nigeria. His parents were devoted Muslims and encouraged their children to follow in their footsteps. Imam made sure that he prayed five times a day according to the teachings in the Quran.

His education was constantly disrupted as his family moved about a lot. Each time the family moved, he had to change schools and that might have been the cause of his average performance at school.

After he completed his secondary education, the family moved to Lagos in search of a better life and Imam enrolled to complete his advanced secondary education. He did not do well enough to obtain the grades needed to gain entry into university. He decided on a polytechnic education instead and even there, he did not do well. He eventually decided to go into business. He was assisted with some money from his parents to start with and was able to build up his business to a decent level – making just about enough to feed his family being a wife and three children.

The problems in the Nigerian economy and the ever-rising cost of living meant that the family constantly struggled financially to make ends meet. His wife who he met when he was in secondary school in his home town in the northern part of Nigeria and who had followed him to Lagos, engaged in petty trade to support the family. Imam knew that the family always had to supplement its income to keep its head above water. He tried to add other sources of income to generate more revenue for the ever-increasing needs of the family. However, his life turned for the worse when one day his first child became very ill. He was diagnosed with sickle cell anaemia and constantly required hospital treatment. Hospital treatment had ceased to be free in Nigeria some time before.

One day, the boy was very ill and was rushed to the hospital for emergency treatment. Imam was told by the doctor that the boy required surgery but before he could be treated, the family needed to pay a substantial amount of money. Imam was faced with a dilemma – he had to decide whether to sell his goods to generate the money required for the treatment which meant that the family would become very poor or he could bring the child home and somehow hope that he would survive. Eventually, he felt he could not bear to continue to watch his son writhe in constant pain and he decided to sell all his merchandise to pay for the treatment. The boy's life was saved but the family had become very poor. The family went into debt as their rent went unpaid and his creditors stopped advancing money to him. He became depressed and desperate and one day after having some drinks, he decided he would end it all and attempted to commit suicide; but that failed. He then started to drink heavily and be-came abusive towards his wife and children.

One day he met Adio at the place he went to go and drink, and he told him his problems. Adio had compassion on him and introduced Imam to the other members of the group and from then on, he started to make enough money to take care of his family. He had hoped that he would soon make enough money from armed robbery to use the money to set up a legal but profitable business.

Meanwhile, Imam stared at the lifeless bodies around him and heaved a great sigh. "I never thought a day like this would come," said Imam. "Well it's come sooner than I thought and we just have to face it."

Priest and Imam looked at each other wearily as if saying to one another; "the end is near."

Imam put down his gun and took off the bullet proof vest he was wearing. Priest stared at him, not knowing what Imam was doing. Imam took out his prayer beads from his pocket. He had always taken the prayer beads with him every time the group went out on robbery operations. It was a kind of lucky charm for him. Priest looked on in amazement. Imam then sat down on the floor.

"What are you doing?" Priest asked Imam.

"I want to ask God for forgiveness of my sins before I die," said Imam.

"If it is because of this job that we are doing, I have not sinned," said Priest. "It is in the Bible, that when a hungry man steals to feed himself, he has not sinned. Only when he is caught is he then required to replace what he has stolen seven fold. It's in … hmm … Proverbs 6: 30–31."

"So, what you are saying is … you are robbing others because you're hungry … eh. Is that what you're saying?" asked Imam.

"I graduated from university like everyone else but I couldn't find a job. My father wanted me to become a priest but I was kicked out of the Convent for breaking the rules. What else could I do," asked Priest.

"So, you are saying that we are robbing others because we are hungry. You built three houses from the money you made from robbing others and you're claiming that you robbed people because you were hungry … Eh …"

"Shut your mouth or I'll shut it for you," Priest said, cocking his gun and pointing it at Imam as if he were about to shoot.

"What … you want to shoot me? You know what your problem is … you! You don't like hearing the truth," said Imam to Priest.

"Keep quiet or I'll shut your mouth for you," said Priest as he raised his gun and pointed it at Imam.

"You want to shoot me? Go ahead. Add me to your sins," said Imam.

Priest also known as Paul was originally from eastern Nigeria but presently resided in Lagos. He was one of five children – two boys and three girls – borne to Mr and Mrs Chukwu. The family were staunch Catholics and attended church regularly. Mr Chukwu was an honest, hardworking family man who did his best to make sure that his children had a better life than he had had. He made sure that his children were brought up in the proper way – to respect authority, fear God and grow up to be somebody in society. A normal day in the Chukwu family home started with a morning prayer, and afterwards, everyone would go about their daily business. The day ended with an evening prayer and everyone went to bed. Mr Chukwu had very high hopes for all his children; and in particular, Paul, whom he hoped would grow up to become a priest. However, Paul from when he was young had always had a problem with authority. He would push boundaries and often got into trouble with his father. His father noticed that and explored many ways to put Paul on the right path.

After Paul finished his primary school education, he started to hang out with the gangs in his area. His father decided to put him into a boarding school away from their local area and away from his usual friends. Even then, his father was often called to meet with the school principal because of Paul's bad behaviour.

Mr Chukwu did not give up on his son however, and prayed fervently that God would change him. He tried his best to teach all his children in the ways of the Lord and he made sure that they always took Holy Communion at church. After a few years in boarding school, it appeared that God had started to answer Mr Chukwu's prayer as, all of a sudden, Paul started to do well in school and was always at the top of his class academically. He successfully completed his secondary school education and obtained very good grades in his General Certificate School Education results, but he had to leave the boarding school to join another school for his advanced level secondary education.

The boarding school he went to did not offer advanced level secondary education. Paul had to find another school to continue his education. He gained admission to a school close to home. At first, he started off well, but unfortunately, towards the end of his education at the new school, he started to rebel against his father's plan for him to become a priest. Paul got involved with some female friends in the area and kicked against the idea of not marrying and devoting one's life entirely to God's work. However, he was scared of his father and couldn't make his feelings known to him. Meanwhile, his father encouraged him to study Theology and after completing his first degree, he gained admission into a convent not far from their home town in Eastern Nigeria; to become a priest. The intake for that year included some beautiful young women and Paul found one of them irresistible. Although the males and females were separated and hardly ever came together except when celebrating mass in the chapel, Paul found a way of befriending one of the nuns and after some time, the two of them started to meet secretly, away from the convent. However, the secret was exposed when she became pregnant and Paul was named as the man responsible. Both were kicked out of the convent and Paul and his father had never spoken to each other since that time. Paul left home but took with him a pocket Bible that his father gave him when he was going into the convent. Paul came to Lagos in search of a job but when he couldn't find a job, he got involved with some area boys who introduced him into gangs and he started to engage in illegal activities. He started with petty robbery like pickpocketing, shoplifting and soon 'graduated' into armed robbery. He later got married and had three children. His mother attended the marriage but his father did not attend. As far as Paul's father was concerned, Paul no longer existed.

Meanwhile, on the bridge, Imam sat down and started to pray. He held the prayer beads in his right hand and appeared to be counting the beads with his fingers while at the same time moving his head back and forth continuously. He was heard muttering a word repeatedly "Astaghfirullah, Astaghfirullah, Astaghfirullah …" Priest watched as Imam continued to pray. Another gun shot came from the police and hit the car close to Imam. Imam did not flinch but continued his prayer. Priest on the other hand ducked and started to return fire.

CHAPTER **6**

The news of Superintendent Jang's death had reached the police station. It was agreed that another senior officer Superintendent James Ezeugo would go over to the scene of the robbery and take over control of the operations.

Superintendent Ezeugo was a mixed-race Nigerian who had lived abroad with his family (wife and two children) before deciding to resettle in Africa, the ancestral home of his father. He was a devoted Christian and family man. He was born in the UK where he received most of his academic education. His father Emeka Ezeugo a black Nigerian met his mother Louise, a white English girl while the former was studying in the UK. They met at the university where both were studying. It was love at first sight. In the beginning, it was difficult as Louise's parents were very much against inter-racial marriage. For a long time, Louise would not bring Emeka home or even mention to her parents that she was in a relationship with a black man. Her parents' first sighting of Emeka was one day when they stopped by at their daughter's university on their way home from a visit to a family friend.

On that day, Emeka happened to be visiting Louise. It was not a planned visit by Louise's parents but road works caused a diversion and they found themselves driving close to their daughter's university, and they decided to make a quick visit. Louise's mobile phone rang and she saw the name of her mother on the phone. She thought they were calling her from home and quickly answered the phone. Her mother asked her where she was and she replied that she was at home on the campus. Louise's mother told her that she and her dad were just passing close to Louise's university and had decided to stop by and were actually waiting at the door outside.

Louise was nervous about what her parents would say but she nevertheless went to open the door for them and they came in. Louise's parents noticed Emeka but did not think much of him. Louise introduced him as her classmate who had been very helpful and supportive towards her. This was true. Emeka is a very brilliant student in class and assisted Louise with her academic work. However, when Louise's parents eventually found out that Emeka was in fact Louise's lover, Louise was already pregnant with Emeka's child. Louise's parents were not very happy about it but felt that their hands were tied and had no option but to accept the state of things. Louise's mum cried when she discovered that her daughter was going out with a black man. Louise's father was very angry and could not bear to look at his daughter's face for a very long time.

Emeka's parents hailed from eastern Nigeria. They lived in a village in Eastern Nigeria and never travelled abroad. Emeka's father was a traditional chief and together with his wife, had high expectations of their only child. As a matter of fact, their plan was that Emeka would return home after completing his education in England and follow in his father's footsteps by taking on his father's chieftaincy title when he died and they were already sounding out a girl among the beautiful young ladies in the village for him to marry. It was important that the wife of whoever held such an important traditional title understood the culture very well and in particular how to relate to her husband's relatives and attend to them during important traditional occasions. Therefore, when Emeka's parents heard that he was engaged to a white woman, they were very disappointed; but nevertheless, accepted their son's marital choice.

Despite their racial differences, Louise and Emeka loved each other very much. This was evident in the way they related to one another whenever they were in each other's company. They could be seen holding hands, caressing each other and even kissing each other in public. This public show of affection was not liked by Emeka. He was brought up in Africa where such behaviour in public is frowned upon; almost seen as a taboo, but he soon realized that this was what Louise wanted and quickly adapted himself to it.

Louise and Emeka successfully completed their university education. Louise passed with a second class upper grading while Emeka got first class. Shortly after completing their university education, they discovered that Louise was pregnant and they got married. The wedding occasion was great. Friends and family members attended. Emeka's parents could not attend as they could not arrange to get their passports and visas on time.

Married life started well as the newlyweds were already expecting their first child. Louise found a job very quickly but Emeka, despite his good academic results, found it difficult to secure a well-paid permanent job. As a result, despite being heavily pregnant, Louise had to work until just few weeks before her expected delivery date as she was the main breadwinner in the family. This situation did not change much after James arrived which put enormous strain on their finances and subsequently on their marriage. The couple started to drift apart as they started arguing and fighting and eventually, they split up. Realising that he might be able to secure a very good job back home in Africa, Emeka decided to return to Nigeria.

James had a very difficult childhood. The break-up of the marriage of his parents did not help his situation either. He was left in the custody of his mother Louise, but his father made regular visits while living in England and ensured that he was not totally cut off from his son's upbringing, although his role was a limited one. James was an average student in school but frequently got into trouble with the school authorities. His mum and dad worked closely together to ensure that his life was not totally derailed. James found it difficult to cope with the racism and rejection he sometimes received within his community. He found it hard to understand why someone that looked like his mum did not treat him like his mum did and, instead, treats him differently to other people. To help him, his father suggested sending him to a secondary school in Nigeria and his mother agreed. This experience helped him a lot. He stayed with his paternal grandparents in the village and enjoyed so much love and acceptance from the people around him which he had not experienced when he was in England. He had fond memories of his time in Nigeria and the friends he had made there. That was what encouraged him to maintain the connection and was one of the reasons why he eventually decided to resettle in Africa.

After James completed his secondary school education in Nigeria, he returned to England for his university education and came out with a second-class honours degree. He later joined Her Majesty's Prison Service as a prison officer and slowly worked his way up to the rank of a senior officer. He met his wife Josephine who was also a Nigerian and a psychologist at the prison where James worked. They had two children, Adam who was eight and Sarah who was five.

Although married and settling in the UK after his university education, James always had it at the back of his mind to eventually return to settle in Nigeria. His experience of racism in the UK, compared to his experience when he went to live with his paternal grandparents, helped to convince him that his future lay in Africa. He always recounted an incident when he was driving in the fairly new Mercedes Benz he had bought not long after he became a senior officer in Her Majesty's Prison Service. At around midday on a week-day he was driving along a street in Northwest London and was flashed by a marked police car to stop. One of the police officers got out of the vehicle and approached his car. James was asked to step out of his car. Out of curiosity, he asked why he was stopped but the reply he got greatly upset him. He was told that his name showed that he was a Nigerian and it was well known that Nigerians were usually involved in fraud. He was angry about that as he felt that it wasn't only that he had been singled out because of the colour of his skin and race but was also told the reason point blank. He was searched and when nothing untoward was found, he was allowed to go. This was in sharp contrast to his experience when he lived in Nigeria where he was treated like a prince.

One day James saw an advert about a recruitment exercise going on within the Nigerian Police Force and he quickly applied. He was offered the job. His experience in the UK Prison Service helped him a lot as he advanced very quickly within the Nigerian Police Force and within a few years he was promoted to the rank of superintendent.

However, James Ezeugo's experience of life in Nigeria when he was young and attending secondary school was different from what he discovered on resettling in Nigeria. There was corruption which was endemic within the system and he found himself having to compromise many of his long-held principles in order to get by in life. He realized that giving bribes was a way of life there and even if you refused to take a bribe, you had to be prepared to give money or else you would find life very difficult. Nevertheless, he maintained his integrity and always ensured that he and other officers serving under him observed the rule of law at all times and resisted the temptation to engage in corruption.

After he was informed that he would be taking over operations on the bridge, Superintendent Ezeugo was briefed about the loss of lives suffered by the police and the need for reinforcements. He then called some officers to take along with him.

"We are going to the bridge north of Lagos," he said to the group of officers standing around him.

"Isn't that the wobbling bridge?" asked one of the officers.

"Well, it is, and apparently there is gunfire raging there at the moment," said Superintendent Ezeugo.

"I don't think this bridge will be standing after this," said another officer.

"The bridge has been wobbling ever since anyone could remember, but it never collapsed," said another officer.

"It's only getting worse," said another.

"My father once told me that the bridge has been wobbling since Colonial days."

"And it has never been repaired?" asked Superintendent Ezeugo.

"Oga! there have been many stories about that bridge. Some said many contracts have been awarded for its repairs and payments made but no work has ever been carried out to repair the bridge."

"There was a rumour that a contract to build a replacement bridge was approved and the funds paid out but we never see any new bridge," added another officer.

"And meanwhile… the condition of the bridge is getting worse, I guess?" asked Superintendent Ezeugo.

"Yes sir," another officer replied.

"I just hope it doesn't collapse when we are on it today," said one of the officers.

"It won't … I'm sure it won't," replied another officer.

On arriving at the scene, Superintendent Ezeugo was updated by the most senior officer around, Sergeant Kenneth about the developments.

"Oga! We don loose five officers already and oga Peter. May his soul rest in peace," reported Kenneth.

"I know. What a waste," Superintendent Ezeugo said. "These are unnecessary deaths."

Superintendent Ezeugo took over the control of the operation and ordered the officers to get into strategic positions. He then asked two of the officers to advance on the position of the robbers. One officer was to move into advance position while the other would start firing in the direction of the robbers as he moved forward. The officers did as they were told.

Meanwhile, Imam continued his prayer as if unconcerned by the events around him. Then the shots started coming in. Priest ducked to avoid being hit. Imam continued praying unmoved by the incoming fire. The intensity of the shots was getting heavier and the frequency increased. Priest knew there could only be one thing happening; the police were advancing on the robbers' position. Priest looked under the car. He was right. He saw what looked like police officers' boots moving towards their position. They were very close. He got his gun ready and moved away slightly. A shot came in. It might have hit something very close but Priest did not know what it was. Priest did not see the shot hit Imam but he noticed blood running from under Imam's hat and down his face. Imam nevertheless continued his prayer. Priest got up quickly and opened fire in the direction of the advancing officers. One of the officers got hit and died instantly. The other advancing officer opened fire on Priest, but the shots hit his bullet proof vest. Priest shot the officer and the officer died instantly.

Superintendent Ezeugo saw the two officers die and said, "These are unnecessary deaths . . .with a helicopter gunship, this hold up would have been ended within minutes. In fact, there won't be a hold up like this on a bridge again because the robbers are not stupid." Just as he was finishing his statement, he saw a helicopter flying in the sky.

"Who requested a helicopter?" Superintendent Ezeugo asked.

"No one sir," Kenneth replied.

"I think it is the inspector general of police sir," said another officer. "He is visiting Lagos today and the helicopter was supposed to be used to carry him to locations that he was scheduled to visit in order to avoid the heavy traffic on the road," added the officer. Superintendent Ezeugo shook his head in disgust.

At the robbers' location, Imam was still praying. "Astaghfirullah, Astaghfirullah, Astaghfirullah ..." He was moving his head forward and backward in prayer mode. He was breathing heavily now as if he was gasping for breath. He might have been hit by gun shots. More shots were coming in now. Another one hit Imam in the chest. Imam moved his head backward but could not bring it down again. He leaned back on the car and breathed his last. Only Priest was left out of the group of armed robbers. Priest turned his head and glanced at Imam. He crouched close to the dead body and used his hand to close Imam's eyes. With his gun in one hand, Priest used his other hand to bring out the pocket-sized Bible he had from his pocket. This was the Bible his father had given him, the day he gained entry into the Convent as a trainee priest.

He looked at the Bible and shaking his head, he asked the question. "God! Why ... why did you fill me with so much greed, that I didn't know when to stop." Priest shook his head again and moved slowly but quietly to within a hand's throw of the sea below. He looked at the pocket Bible once again and said, "This is it. I won't be needing this where I'm going." He threw the Bible over the bridge and into the sea below. He checked his gun to make sure it was fully loaded.

Priest got up from where he had been crouching and advanced towards the police. He threw all caution into the wind and started shooting as he moved forward. Priest's action took the police by surprise and several officers were hit. The police returned fire and there was a barrage of shots directed towards Priest. He kept going forward, as many of the shots only hit the bullet proof vest he was wearing. One of the incoming shots hit his thigh and then another hit his leg. Priest slumped on his knees, but still contin-ued to shoot. Another shot hit his hand and another hit the gun, making it fly out of his hand. A barrage of shots rained down on Priest. After a while, he fell face down and died.

Superintendent Ezeugo gestured to the officers to stop shoot-ing. After few minutes and as there was no more incoming fire from the robbers, Superintendent Ezeugo sent two of the officers to check and make sure that there were no armed robbers left. The two officers confirmed that all the armed robbers were dead and there were none left. Superintendent Ezeugo then looked around and saw several officers lying around him – some were injured but many were dead.

He sighed and muttered. "These are unnecessary deaths. I am leaving the force." He was however heard by Sergeant Kenneth who stood beside him and fortunately had escaped uninjured.

"Oga please! Make you no leave. We need honest people like you in the force sir," pleaded Sergeant Kenneth.

"I'm returning to the UK with my family," said Superintendent Ezeugo.

"Oga! Remember why you left the UK in the first place. Everyone loves you here," pleaded Kenneth. Many officers at the police station where Superintendent James Ezeugo worked had heard about his life story when he was in the UK.

Meanwhile, once he had made sure that the armed robbers were all dead, Superintendent James Ezeugo ordered that the injured officers be taken to hospital and the corpses of the dead officers and robbers be removed to the morgue. He then returned with the remaining officers to the police station.

CHAPTER **7**

In the late afternoon, just as Mrs Jang was getting ready to drive to her children's school to pick them up, she noticed a police vehicle driving towards her house which stopped just in front of her house and blocked her driveway. She saw two senior officers – a male and a female getting out of the vehicle, but she did not see her husband. The look on their faces showed that the news was not good. Mrs Jang who had already entered her car and started the engine immediately turned the engine off and stepped out of her car.

"Is everything okay? Where is my husband?" she asked.

"Good afternoon madam," said one of the officers.

"Where is my husband?" repeated Mrs Jang.

"Shall we go inside?" asked one of the officers.

Mrs Jang started to shake and sweat profusely. She tried to open the door but the keys fell from her hand. One of the officers stooped low and retrieved the keys for her. Mrs Jang took the keys and opened the front door and they all went in. She immediately asked the question again. "Where is my husband?"

"Please sit down madam," said the female officer. Mrs Jang refused to sit down and barked out the question. "Where is my husband?"

"Sorry madam. There was an armed robbery on the bridge. He was in charge of the operation but was shot by the robbers and … he … he died." Mrs Jang collapsed at hearing the news of the death of her husband. The two officers quickly came to her aid. She was lifted from the floor where she was lying and put on a chair to sit. Mrs Jang started to cry and shake uncontrollably.

"I'm sorry madam," said one of the officers.

Mrs Jang continued to cry whilst the two officers sat down quietly. Mrs Jang explained that she was just about to go and pick up the children from school and she was at a loss what to tell them about their dad. One of the police officers offered to help Mrs

Jang pick up the children from school. Mrs Jang agreed and rang the school to let them know. Her voice was shaking when she spoke to the school. She didn't tell the school what had happened. She only informed the school that something had happened and that she would not be able to pick the children up herself. It was agreed that the female officer should stay behind with Mrs Jang while the male officer took the police car to go and pick up the children. Mrs Jang told the school the name of the officer who would be picking up the children. After the male officer had left, the female officer asked about other family members who needed to be contacted and who could also offer emotional support to Mrs Jang and her family. Mrs Jang spoke about Superintendent Jang's mother and other relatives, but she said she would contact them herself. After bringing the children home from school, the officers stayed a while with the family and then they left.

After Superintendent Jang's body was released for burial, the Nigeria Police Force offered to give him a state burial and the family agreed. On the morning of the burial, Mrs Jang was dressed in all-black attire with a black hat. The children wore black suits. The family were picked up at home in a police vehicle and driven to the police barracks where the police chapel was situated. This was where the funeral ceremony would take place. Mrs Jang and the children sat in the front row flanked by family members. Superintendent Jang's mother did not attend the funeral. In the next row were senior police officers and a representative of the state police commissioner. The chapel was filled with other officers and members of the public, together with other family members and friends who had come to pay their last respects. Among the congregation was Superintendent Jang's mistress Aunty Esther who was also dressed in black with a black hat. There was no official recognition for being a mistress. She was only known to a few officers who were very close to Superintendent Jang but not to any of Superintendent Jang's family members. In fact, only a few close friends and associates of the late Superintendent Jang acknowledged and went to greet her.

The chaplain leading the service signalled for the congregation to stand up as the coffin bearing Superintendent Jang's body was brought in by uniformed police officers. Mrs Jang put on her black shade to hide her tears. The children started to cry as the coffin reached the front of the chapel. Mrs Jang held the hand of the youngest child – a five-year-old girl who was very close to her dad. They all called her daddy's little princess. She was the only daughter. The other three children were boys.

The chaplain said the opening prayer and it was followed by the opening hymn. One of Superintendent Jang's children read the first Bible passage. There was a little sermon followed by a message from the representative of the state commissioner of police. The oldest of Superintendent Jang's children came forward and spoke about his father. He described his father as a dedicated family man who was always there for his family and in particular for his children. He was the main and the only bread winner in the family. The mother did not have to work. On hearing the eulogy from her son, Mrs Jang wiped a few tears from her eyes with the white handkerchief she was holding. The son filled with emotion paused a little bit as he tried though unsuccessfully to hold back the tears. Afterwards, Superintendent Ezeugo who had taken over the control of the operation on the bridge following the fatal shooting of Superintendent Jang came forward and made a speech about the life and work of the late Superintendent Jang. He knew Superintendent Jang very well as they attended police college at the same time. Superintendent James Ezeugo told what a valiant, hardworking and dedicated officer late Superintendent Jang was. He described how he was always giving his best over and above the call of duty despite the limited resources at his disposal. As he finished his speech, the congregation stood up and clapped.

The funeral service came to an end. The congregation stood up as the coffin containing the corpse of late Superintendent Jang was hoisted up by the group of officers who had brought it in earlier. The congregation remained standing as the bearers of the coffin moved steadily towards the exit of the chapel. As the coffin got to where Aunty Esther stood, she took out the handkerchief in her bag and wiped away tears from her eyes.

"He died for me," she murmured. "He died for me," she repeated.

A well-dressed gentleman standing beside her heard what Aunty Esther said and asked, "Were you also on the bridge?"

Aunty Esther repeated, "He died for me," as she sobbed uncontrollably.

The well-dressed man beside her asked the question again. "Were you on the bridge?"

The man standing on the other side of Aunty Esther replied, "He died for everyone … for all of us … for everything … the good and the bad in our society."

The coffin containing Superintendent Jang's body was driven by a hearse, followed by the official car carrying the late Superintendent Jang's wife and the children. Other vehicles carrying the other family members were followed by the vehicles carrying the chaplain and other senior members of the police force and other police officers and then the congregation. Superintendent Jang's body was laid to rest at a nearby cemetery.

The author

Folorunso G. Makinde was born in Lagos, Nigeria where he completed his Primary School education. He also attended Ilora Baptist Grammar School and Olivet Baptist High School both in Oyo State, Nigeria before moving to London in the UK in 1986. He is a self-employed lawyer, who is a solicitor registered with the Law Society of England and Wales. He enjoys watching documentaries and programmes on current affairs. He founded Nigerians For Referendum. He is married with three children. His authorial career includes articles on political issues in Nigeria, and he is published on the Nigerian Masterweb.